Chantalle Edmunds hails from the North East of England and is a history graduate who has built a successful career as a broadcast journalist, having worked in the UK, Washington D.C. and New York. She lives in London with her husband, two children and two cats.

JUST  THE JOB FOR GEORGE

Chantalle Edmunds

To Matilda and Sadie
Happy Reading!
Chantalle Edmunds

AUSTIN MACAULEY PUBLISHERS™

LONDON • CAMBRIDGE • NEW YORK • SHARJAH

Copyright © Chantalle Edmunds (2021)

A CIP catalogue record for this title is available from the British Library.

ISBN 9781528977616 (Paperback)
ISBN 9781528977937 (Hardback)
ISBN 9781398427822 (ePub e-book)

www.austinmacauley.com

First Published (2021)
Austin Macauley Publishers Ltd
25 Canada Square
Canary Wharf
London
E14 5LQ

This book is dedicated to my daughter who helped visualize what George would have looked like, to my son, who laughed wholeheartedly at the story and to my husband who never lost belief in me.

George was a dragon slayer,
He'd been one for many years
And everyone in the country
Called him saint or sir.

He'd defeated the dragon Brimstone
Who'd spread terror across the land.
He'd used his trusty lance and sword
Beating him with just one hand.

George had set up a hotline
For anyone to report
If a dragon was *in* their neighbourhood
And needed to be caught.

But *in* five long years the phone hadn't rung
There weren't any dragons about.
None *in* the villages, towns and cities
That George could go and sort out.

His wife Holly shook her head,
"George, I think it's time.
You need to find another job
You've got to toe the line."

George said: "What shall I do?
I've got no other skills
Defeating dragons is all I know
And even that can't pay the bills."

That night as he lay in bed
George tossed and turned.
All other regular jobs
Seemed a bit absurd.

As the light crept in the room
George sat up in bed.
"I've got it," he nudged Holly
And with a wink he said,

"I'll set up a laundry business
And I'll use my lance
It'll make a brilliant washing line
If I'm given half a chance."

George called his next door neighbours,
Mr McGee and Mrs Slee.
"I'm setting up a laundry business
Would you be interested for a fee?"

Shirts, sheets and nappies,
George collected them all
But compared to fighting dragons
He felt a little small.

The washing machine frothed and bubbled
And soon all the laundry was done.
"Quick Holly," shouted George,
Come and see how I've got on."

"Look at this shirt, it's tangled with a nappy
And these trousers have shrunk in size.
Seeing all this, George, your customers
Aren't in for a nice surprise."

They were sitting in the garden
When George came up with a new plan
"The window cleaner's moved away,
I'll be the replacement man."

George's first job was cleaning the church.
The windows were very high.
With a cloth on his lance he pointed it
Towards the bright blue sky.

With a flick of the wrist, he skilfully cleaned
The stained glass windows first.
Only one remained, but George soon
Found this was by far the worst.

It was on an odd angle, so George had to
Stand right on his tippy toes.
One little wobble was all it took
And glass fell on his nose.

The vicar came rushing out.
"What was that awful clatter?
I was just talking to the church band
When I heard something shatter."

Holly shouted from the door
When George came wandering back.
"I hear Reverend Jefferson
Thought her church was under attack."

George went outside with his lance
Flexing it against the ground.
He looked at the fence, then at the trees
And turned himself around.

He gripped the lance with all his might.
The fence looked very tall
But George was sure he could get
Over it without a nasty fall.

George landed in next door's garden
Right behind Mrs Slee
Who was examining her petunias
Crouching down on one knee.

"Heavens alive!" she shouted.
"What an awful shock.
Have you come to collect more washing?
I'd prefer it if you'd knock."

George felt triumphant
He'd made it over the fence.
A career in pole vaulting?
Suddenly it all made sense.

So George started training
At a sporting ground.
His coaches thought he was very good
And word soon got around.

He'd won every competition
And could pole vault over trees
It was time for something bigger
That would give him better fees.

The village church had a spire
The tallest in the land.
It would be a challenge
But George had it all in hand.

Beside the church the villagers
Had put a trampoline
George would have to land on it
To avoid a nasty scene.

The crowd held their breath
As he travelled very fast.
Would he come back down to earth?
Could his new luck last?

"Bulls eye!" George shouted.
As he sprung high in the air
"Have I set a new record
That wasn't already there?"

Everyone in the village
Came to shake his hand.
"Now," said Holly. "You'll be known
As the best pole vaulter in the land."

George went on collecting trophies
And he proudly displayed them all
But one Sunday over dinner
There was an unexpected call . . .